Be careful.
Don't think these
little children
are worth nothing.
I tell you that
they have
angels in heaven
who are always
with my Father
in Heaven.

MATTHEW 18:10.

Tree Forts and Trumpets

Featuring G.T. and the Halo Express,
created by Doug and Debbie Kingsriter

Written by Ann Hibbard
Illustrated by Ann Neilsen

Published by Focus on the Family Publishing
Pomona, CA 91799

Distributed by Word Books, Dallas, Texas. Copyright © 1990 Focus on the Family Publishing
Scriptures quoted from *The Everyday Bible, New Century Version,* copyright © 1987, 1988 by
Word Publishing, Dallas, Texas 75039. Used by permission.
G.T. and the Halo Express, Michael, Christy and Billy Baxter
are copyrighted
by Doug and Debbie Kingsriter ©1987.
No part of this book may be reproduced or copied without written permission of the publisher.

Library of Congress Catalog Card Number 90-081107
ISBN 0-929608-21-6
Cassette tapes featuring G.T. and the Halo Express in other adventures are also available by contacting
King Communications, P.O. Box 24472, Minneapolis, MN 55424 or your local Christian bookstore.

Michael jumped on his bike and took off down the street. With a squeal of the tires, he brought the bike to a screeching stop beside two boys.

"Hi, guys!" Michael said. "What's up?"

"I'm starting a club," announced Billy Baxter, a tall, tough-looking boy. "You guys can join, if you obey my orders."

"Sure, Billy," said the other boy, Bubba. He pursed his lips and began to blow a bubble with the gum he was chewing. His cheeks puffed out, and he looked just like one of the three little pigs. The bubble popped, and Bubba pulled the gum back inside his mouth with a snap.

"What kind of a club?" Michael questioned.

"A tree fort club," answered Billy with an air of importance. "My dad made me the most incredible tree fort you've ever seen."

"Incredible," Bubba echoed, nodding and snapping his gum.

"And only club members are allowed up in it," Billy stated. "You've gotta be cool to be in my club. So, Michael, are you in or out?"

"Yeah, I'll be in your club," Michael agreed.

The sound of a skateboard drew their attention up the street. They didn't recognize the kid on the skateboard, but he looked about their age.

He zigzagged toward them, picking up speed as he skated down the hill. Suddenly he made the skateboard jump. He and his skateboard did a complete somersault in midair.

"That kid must have wings!" breathed Billy.

"Maybe he'd like to join our club," suggested Michael.

"Hey, I'm the leader. I decide who's in the club and who's not," Billy declared.

The new kid landed perfectly and rolled to a stop in front of them.

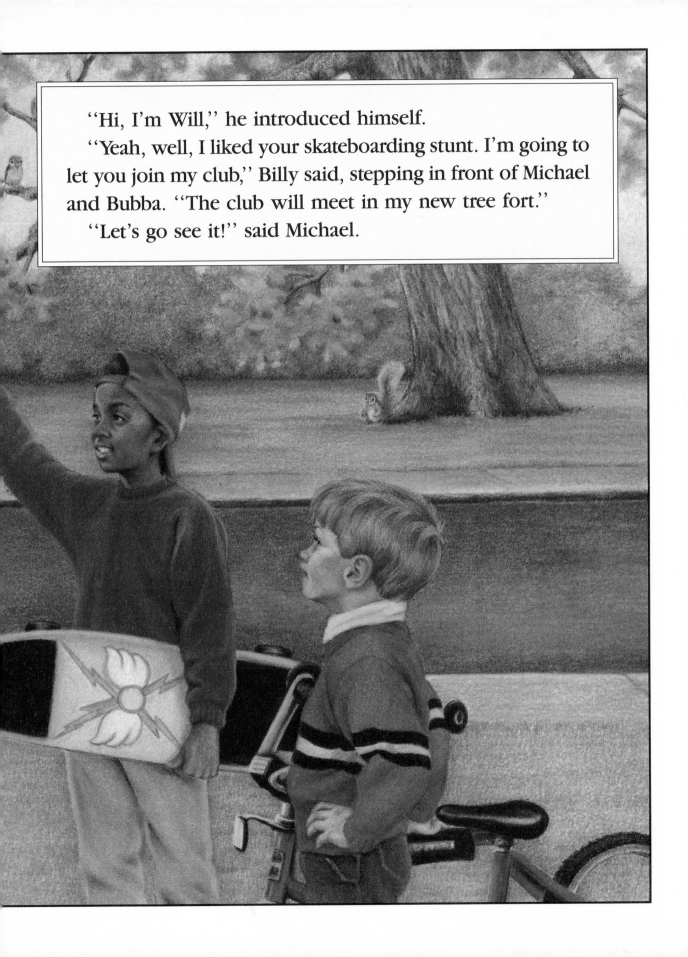

"Hi, I'm Will," he introduced himself.

"Yeah, well, I liked your skateboarding stunt. I'm going to let you join my club," Billy said, stepping in front of Michael and Bubba. "The club will meet in my new tree fort."

"Let's go see it!" said Michael.

The four boys sprinted to Billy's backyard. High in the branches of a tall, sturdy oak tree was the tree fort. It had a peaked roof with real shingles on it, big, open windows, and a rope ladder hanging down from the doorway. Painted brown, the fort seemed to disappear in the branches. You wouldn't even know it was there if you didn't see the rope ladder.

"Wow!" exclaimed Michael and Will.

Bubba stared up at the tree fort and popped another piece of gum in his already-full mouth. Billy just stood there with his arms folded across his chest, looking proud.

"What are we waiting for?" cried Michael as he made a dash for the rope ladder.

The boys clambered up the rope like four-legged spiders. Once inside, they saw the tree fort was even better than they had imagined. A small table with a couple of benches and a big, comfy bean-bag chair seemed to invite them to stay a long time. Sunlight streamed in the two windows.

"Wow, you can see the whole neighborhood from up here!" exclaimed Michael, looking out one of the windows.

"Incredible!" said Bubba between chomps.

Billy Baxter plopped down in the bean-bag chair.

"All right, guys, let's get started," he said in his take-charge voice. "I've got a plan."

"Yeah? What is it?" asked Michael, leaning forward eagerly.

"The tree fort is a castle, see," Billy began. "And I'm the king. Bubba, here, can be my royal prince, and you two can be the guards."

"That's cool," responded Will. "Hey, maybe I could be the herald. You know, the guy who goes before the king and blows the trumpet."

Will put his hands up as if he were holding an invisible trumpet. Then he put his lips together and blew. "DOOT-do-do-DOOO!" To the boys' amazement, Will sounded exactly like a real trumpet.

"How did you do that?" gasped Michael.

"It's all in the blowing, sort of like bubble gum," Will answered with a grin. The other boys laughed. Billy's laugh sounded like popcorn exploding in a popcorn popper.

"So what are we supposed to do, Billy?" Michael asked.

"You can start by calling me 'Your Highness,'" Billy said with a scowl. "You must all bow before me and say, 'Yes, Your Highness.'"

Michael, Will and Bubba stood up and bowed in Billy's direction. But they were standing too close, and their heads all bumped together. They crashed to the floor, roaring with laughter.

Billy rose to his feet, looking angry. "This is no time for fooling around. Our enemy could be planning his attack right now."

"What enemy?" Michael asked, quickly adding, "Er, Your Highness."

"There he is," Billy said, pointing out the window. The other boys crowded around.

"That's no enemy. It's just ol' Warren Pleats," Michael said.

"Warren the Wimp, you mean," said Bubba.

"He is Wicked Warren, King of the Wimps," Billy stated. "And he is our enemy. Hey, I've got an idea. Bubba, come with me. Michael and Will, you wait here and protect the castle from Warren, King of the Wimps."

Billy and Bubba climbed down the rope ladder and headed toward the house, talking in low tones. Will turned to Michael.

"So, Michael, what does Billy have against Warren?" Will asked.

"I don't know," Michael answered with a shrug. "I guess Billy's cool and Warren's not."

"What's so *un*cool about Warren?"

"It's hard to explain. He's just different, that's all."

"I don't get it," Will said, shaking his head. "We're all different."

"Yeah, I guess you're right," Michael said.

Then Will's face brightened as if he had just had an idea.

"You want to get a better look at the neighborhood from up here?" Will asked.

"Sure," Michael replied.

Will reached under his sweater and pulled out a big pair of binoculars.

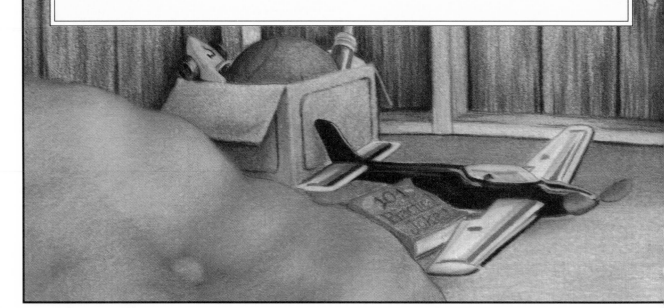

"Wow!" breathed Michael. "How did you fit those under your sweater?"

Will just smiled and shrugged. He lifted the binoculars up to his eyes and adjusted them. Then he handed them to Michael.

"I can't believe it!" Michael exclaimed. "It's like I'm right next to the street!"

Michael scanned the neighborhood. Everything looked huge.

"Wait a minute!" Michael cried out. "I can see Billy and Bubba through the window in Billy's kitchen. Billy is talking on the phone. And Bubba's got something—it looks like a picnic jug. Hey, maybe they're getting some lemonade or something! Now Billy is hanging up. They're leaving. Here they come!"

Michael returned the binoculars to Will, who tucked them back inside his sweater.

Sure enough, Billy and Bubba each toted a heavy-looking picnic jug. Slowly, carefully, they mounted the rope ladder. Finally their heads appeared in the doorway. They plopped the jugs on the floor and pulled themselves in. Billy immediately turned around and hauled up the rope ladder after them. Bubba carried the jugs over to the window and unscrewed the lids.

"Great idea, Your Highness! I'm dying of thirst!" exclaimed Michael. "So where are the cups?"

Billy rolled his eyes. "This isn't for us to drink, dummy. It's ammunition. You know, weapons."

"What's going on?" Michael questioned.

Billy's lips curled in an evil grin. "I've invited our enemy over for a little surprise." He laughed his popcorn popper laugh again, but this time it had a creepy sound to it.

"What are you talking about?" Michael asked suspiciously.

"Shhh!" hissed Bubba. "Here he comes!"

Michael moved over to the window. Down below he saw Warren rounding the corner of Billy's house. Warren glanced around Billy's backyard with an uncertain expression on his face.

Finally Warren stood directly under the tree fort. He gazed around the yard as if he were waiting for someone, but he never once looked up. Michael realized that Warren didn't know that they were up in the tree fort. Warren didn't even know there was a tree fort!

In a flash, Michael saw what was happening. Billy was playing a terrible trick on Warren. Billy and Bubba had already lifted up the jugs of water.

"Warren! Watch out!" Michael screamed.

Warren looked up in surprise—just in time to get his face full of water. His glasses were like two big puddles. He gasped as the cold water ran from his hair down his clothes.

Billy and Bubba dropped onto the floor of the tree fort, laughing and pounding the floor with their fists. Bubba laughed so hard his gum flew out of his mouth.

Warren's face grew beet red. Without saying a word, he turned and walked away.

"That was mean!" shouted Michael.

"Poor little Warren," Billy said sarcastically.

"What's Warren ever done to you?" Michael demanded.

"I didn't know you and Wimpy Warren were such good buddies," Billy said.

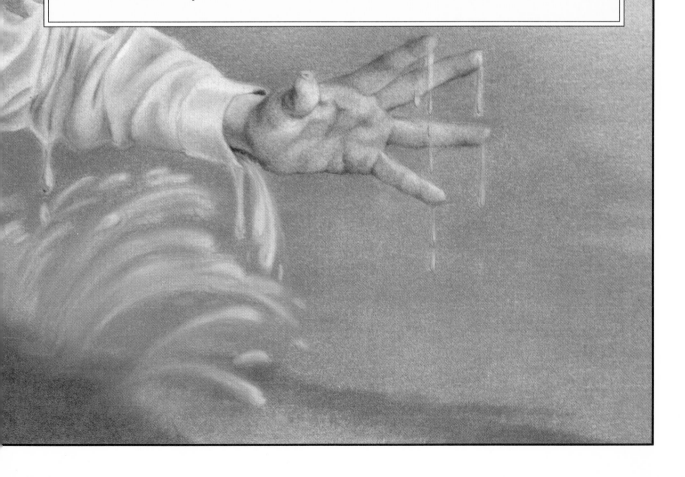

Michael glanced over at Will. Will gave him the "thumbs up" sign and nodded. Michael took a deep breath.

"Look, Billy," he said, "thanks for inviting me to be in your club, but I don't think I want to be in it anymore. So, I'll see you 'round, okay?"

Billy and Bubba exchanged looks of astonishment as Michael threw down the rope ladder and slipped out the doorway.

"I'm with you, Michael," called Will. He slid down the ladder so fast that he somehow made it to the ground before Michael.

"I think I'll go over to Warren's and see how he's doing," Michael told Will.

"That's cool," said Will. "It took a lot of guts for you to stand up for Warren like that."

Michael looked down and dug the toe of his tennis shoe in the dirt. "I haven't been very nice to Warren either."

"I'd say you've made a good start," said Will.

"Hey, maybe the three of us could form a club," Michael burst out. "A club where everyone is welcome."

"Great idea!" agreed Will. He looked behind Michael and exclaimed, "Hi, Good Tidings!"

Michael turned. There stood Michael's angel-friend, G.T., with a smile that reached from ear to ear.

"Hi, Michael! Hi, Will!" G.T. greeted them.

"G.T., you know Will?" Michael asked.

"Sure do!" G.T. responded with a chuckle.

Will pulled off his baseball cap and out popped a shiny, golden halo. Then he took off his sweater, and two white angel wings unfolded behind him.

"You mean, Will's an angel, too?" asked Michael in amazement.

"You bet! In fact, Will goes on special assignments for God," G.T. answered. "He visits earth in disguise to help people like you do God's will."

"When I'm not playing trumpet in G.T.'s band of angels, the Halo Express," Will said with a laugh. Out from behind his back he drew a big golden trumpet.

Then, jumping onto his skateboard, he lifted the trumpet to his lips and began to play. He skateboarded to the music, looping and spinning in the air. And the sound that came from his trumpet was—well, simply divine.

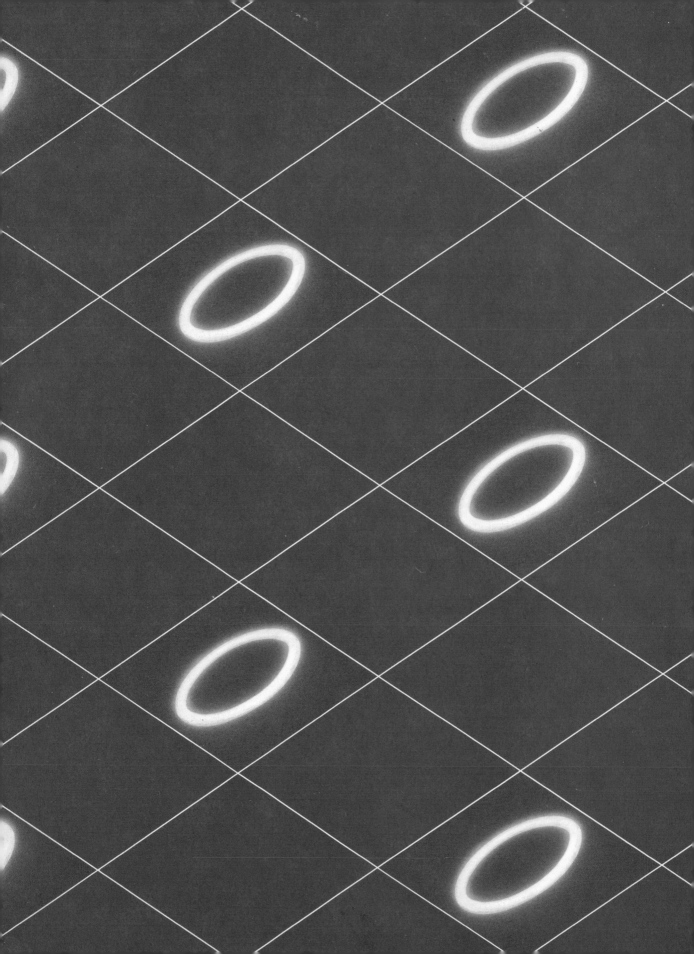